Tots TV Annual

Contents

© 1997 Ragdoll Productions (UK) Ltd.
Design of Tots TV characters & house
© Ragdoll Productions (UK) Ltd. 1993
Tots TV Programmes © Carlton Television Ltd.
MCMXCVII

Annual devised & written by David Moore
Designed by John Timms
Illustrated by Jonathan Mitchell & Tudor Reece
Coloured by Daniel Keay

Published by Grandreams Ltd,
435/437 Edgware Road, Little Venice, London W2 1TH

Ragdoll
works for children

CARLTON

£5.75

This is my secret letter.

I hope you like our secret book. It's all about parties and things. I hope you like it.

I like having parties because then I can eat lots of jelly. I'm going to share this jelly with Tom and Tilly. But I think I might just eat a little bit myself first. Shshshsh.

I like jelly best of all,
When it's in my tummy,
Yum, yum, yum, yum,
Yummy, yummy, yummy.

Love,
    Tiny xx
P.S. Don't tell
    anyone!

Bonjour!
J'aime Tiny et j'aime Tom.
Regarde mon image de
Donkey.

Bisous
Tilly

I am Tom I am.

I have made up a special rhyme especially for you.

I love Tiny,
And I love Tilly,
I love playing games,
And jokes that are silly,
I love my trousers,
And I love jelly,
I love Donkey,
Even though he is a bit SMELLY!

Pooooh! Ha ha ha!

I love you I do.

Tom Tom Tiddle-I-Pom
X X X X X X

P.S. Here is my best ever picture of me

Hello Hippo!

BOOO!

Hippos Are Big And Heavy. When they walk, they don't tiptOE they go BOOM! BOOM! BOOM!

All the Animals ON OUR Lovely Ark.

I Love Donkey. I do.

Me (with a JAM Sandwich ON MY head). XX 7

Right in the middle of a wood, where nobody thinks of looking, where the bracken grows high and the trees grow close together, there's a little yellow house.

It's not very big,
It's not very new,
But this house is magic.

This is the house where Tilly, Tom and Tiny live with their friend Donkey.

(Naughty Furryboo lives there too but that's a secret.)

They all live together in their magic secret house, and nobody sees, and nobody knows...

1. Sometimes Tom just likes to find a nice quiet place to sit and read a book.
One sunny day,
he felt like doing just that.

2. Tom had settled down on a comfy log when,
suddenly,
he heard a noise.
"Tommy Tom Tom!"
It was Tiny.
"Pssst! Tom! Over here!"

Tiny had some leaves in his hair and was hiding behind a bush.

3. "Pssst! Tom!"
"What is it, Tiny?" said Tom. "I'm trying to read my book."
"I'm hiding, Tom!" said Tiny.

4. "I'm playing at hiding," said Tiny. "Tilly is looking for me. You won't tell her where I am, will you?"

"Er... No Tiny, I won't," said Tom, "because I'm just going to sit here quietly and read my book."

"All right then Tom," said Tiny, and he ducked back down behind the bush.

5. "Tom?" said the bush.

"What is it now, Tiny?" said Tom, getting a little bit annoyed.

"You can't see me can you?" said the bush.

"No Tiny, I can't see you at all," said Tom, hardly bothering to look up from his book.

6. Just then, Tilly came along, playing a sunny, hide-and-seek day tune on her flute.

7. "Bonjour Tom!" said Tilly. "Hello Tilly," said Tom. "Est-ce que tu as vu Tiny?" "No, I haven't seen Tiny, thank you very much Tilly, I'm sitting here quietly and reading my book, all right?"

8. Suddenly, a bush not very far away gave a little giggle. "Écoutez!" said Tilly.

9. "Boo!" said Tiny, popping out of his hiding place. "You found me, Tilly.
Now it's your turn to hide!"
Tom sighed.
"Do you mind, Tots," said Tom.
"Just go and play your
hide-and-seek game
somewhere else, please,
because I was here first
and I want to read my
book all nice and
quietly and everything,
all right?"

10. Tilly looked at Tiny, and Tiny looked at Tilly.
"All right then, Tom," said Tiny. "We didn't mean to disturb you.
Your turn to hide, Tilly! I'll stand and look at this tree for a bit while you hide."

11. Tilly ran off into the woods and Tiny began to count loudly.

12. "If there isn't a nice quiet place for me to read my book today," said Tom, "then I'm going to make one!" So that's what he did.

13. Tom settled down with his book in his secret, nice, quiet place. "That's better," he said. "All lovely and quiet. Now I can read my book in peace."

14. Tom read for a bit.

15. Then he ate a biscuit.

16. But after a while, Tom began to feel a little bit lonely. Just then Tilly and Tiny came along.

17. "This," said Tom, "is my secret, nice, quiet place. Would you like to come inside and have a look?" "Oh oui, s'il te plaît," said Tilly. "Yes please!" said Tiny.

18. "There're some books to read here, and a jigsaw to do there," explained Tom. "And some biscuits and things in case we get a little bit hungry."

19. "Cor! What a brilliant, nice, quiet place!" said Tiny.
"I wanted a nice quiet place, Tiny," said Tom. "But I'm glad you're here to share it with me now."

20. Tilly played a nice, quiet place tune on her flute and Tom made up a song to go with it.

21. Sometimes, all I want is a quiet place to hide, So when I want to read my book, I can sit inside. But if I'm feeling lonely, it's nice that I can share my nice quiet place with my best friends, because they're always there.

22. "I love you, I do, Tots," said Tom, and he gave Tiny and Tilly a big hug.

Tots Picture Painting Show

Tilly didn't know what to draw one day. Tiny had an idea.
"I know!" said Tiny. "Why don't you paint my favourite thing ever?"

"Une banane?" asked Tilly.
"No, not a banana, Tilly," laughed Tiny.
"Donkey?" guessed Tilly again.
"No, not Donkey," said Tiny.
"Why don't you
draw my cardigan?"

"Oh! oui, excellent!"
said Tilly, and she set to
work straight away with
her green crayon.

3. "Do you need me to take it off, so you can see better?" asked Tiny, turning round so Tilly could see every bit of his cardigan. "Non," said Tilly, who was concentrating very hard on getting the right number of buttons.

4. "Voilà!" said Tilly, when she had finished. "Brilliant!" said Tiny.

5. "Don't forget the badges," said Tiny.

6. But Tilly didn't want to stop drawing. Next she painted the magic bag. "Sac magique!" said Tilly.

7. Then she drew Tom's trousers. "Lovely, Tilly!" said Tom.

8. She drew round her hands with a crayon to draw some gloves.

9. She even painted some Wellington boots. By lunchtime, Tilly had drawn so many pictures she didn't know where to put them all.

10. Tom had an idea. He strung a piece of string across the room, then he got the clothes pegs from out of the cupboard under the stairs.

11. Then Tom pegged all of Tilly's brilliant pictures on to the line. "There," said Tom, proudly. "Tilly's very own, special picture painting show."

2. Tom and Tiny
gave Tilly
a big hug.
"Brilliant!"
said Tiny.

Make your own washing-line picture show.

You can hang your paintings and drawings up wherever you like!

19

The Mysterious Magic Trail Adventure

Tom and Tiny were sitting at the table in their secret house, about to have their breakfast.
"Tiny," said Tom.
"Have you eaten my toast?"
"No, Tom," said Tiny.
"That's funny," said Tom.

Up in the rafters, Furryboo was having his breakfast.

Just then, Tiny noticed something.
"Tom," said Tiny.
"I think there's definitely something missing."
"What's that, Tiny?" said Tom.
"Where is Tilly this morning?" asked Tiny.

Suddenly, there was a knock at the door.   Rat - a - tat - tat!

"Rat a tat tat! What's that on the mat?" said Tom and Tiny together. Tiny jumped up and went to have a look. There were two envelopes, a blue one and a green one.

I think that green envelope must be for you, tiny Tiny," said Tom,
because green is your favourite colour, it is."
Then that blue one must be for you,
ommy Tom," said Tiny,
because I know that
lue is your
avourite colour."

Tom and Tiny opened their envelopes.
nside each envelope was a piece of paper. On each piece of paper were
some blue blobs and some green blobs and some brown blobs and a long
brown line. On Tom's piece of paper there was a big red "X" as well.

Tiny looked at his picture. Then he looked at it again. Then he turned it upside
down and looked at it. But he still couldn't see what it was.
"That," said Tiny, "is very VERY mysterious."
"It's a mystery!" said Tom.

Just then, Tom had an idea. He put the two pieces of paper together.
"Ah ha!" said Tom. "This... is a treasure map, it is."
"Treasure!" said Tiny. "Brilliant!"
"I think, Tiny, that we have to follow this brown line here, right,
and see where it takes us."
"What an exciting mystery adventure!" said Tiny.

Tom and Tiny put on their coats and pulled on their Wellington boots.
"All ready for a mysterious treasure map adventure mystery!"
said Tiny. And off they went.

Tom made up a song as they set off:

We're going on a treasure hunt,
I wonder what we'll see?
We're following our treasure map,
What will the treasure be?

"Right then," said Tom.
"The map says
we have to go
under the cart."

"Under the cart, Tommy Tom?"
"Yes, Tiny," said Tom.

Tom and Tiny
wriggled
under the cart...

...and out the
other side.

A bit further along
they came to the woodpile.
"What next, Tommy Tom?" said Tiny.
"Right," said Tom.
"Over the woodpile."
"Over the woodpile, Tom?"
asked Tiny.
"Yes, over the woodpile,"
said Tom. "That's what
the map says."

23

Tiny and Tom wibbled
and wobbled...

We're going on a treasure hunt,
I wonder what we'll see?
We're following our treasure map,
What will the treasure be?

...and stumbled right
over the log pile.

A bit further on they came to a
big muddy puddle where Tiny
had been digging.

"The map says
that we have to go through
the muddy puddle," said Tom.
"Right through the middle?"
asked Tiny.
"Er... yes!" said Tom.
"Come on then!"
said Tiny.

Slurp slurp
splish splash splosh,
Tiny and Tom squelched
their Wellington boots...

...right through the middle of the   muddy puddle.

A bit further along they saw their friend Donkey.

"Hello Donkey!" said Tiny.
"We're looking for some extra special treasure."
"And I think our treasure must be right
around here!" said Tom.
"I wonder what the treasure is?"
said Tiny.

ust then, Tom and Tiny
eard a magic trill
rom behind Donkey's shed.

Bonjour Tom! Bonjour Tiny!"
t was Tilly!
Tilly," said Tom. "We liked
ollowing your treasure map!"

Tilly had prepared a special,
urprise breakfast in the woods
or the Tots. Tom and Tiny were
ungry after all
hat wiggling,
vobbling and
squelching.

"What a brilliant
surprise!" said Tiny.
"Ee-aw!" said Donkey.

25

Tots Treasure!

Tiny's tiny treasure game

See how many tiny things
you can squeeze into a small box.
You can only have ONE
of each thing.

"I've written my name
on my little box."

Tilly's noisy treasure.

Find a few small
empty boxes.
Fill each one
with a different thing:
peanuts, rice,
sugar or pebbles.
Ask your friends
to shake the boxes
and try to guess what's
inside each one.

"Écoutez!"

Tom's secret treasure chest.

Find a box with a lid and paint it your favourite colour,
or you could cover it with coloured paper
or pages from an old magazine.
Decorate your box with stickers, glitter, buttons or wool.
This is now your very own secret treasure chest!
Put some of your favourite, secret things in your box
and hide it in a special place.
Secret treasure!

"I've got
a really big conker
and some blue wool.
But don't tell anyone
- it's a secret!"

I love snails...

...One hour later.

Snails move really, really

When Tilly was feeling a bit sad,

We made her a
really excellent
rocket.

Tom and Tilly are my
best friends in the World
ever. I love Tom and Tilly

28

Me and my brilliant box.

Sometimes Tilly stays in bed for ages and ages and ages.

He y there! Lovely cow.

One day...

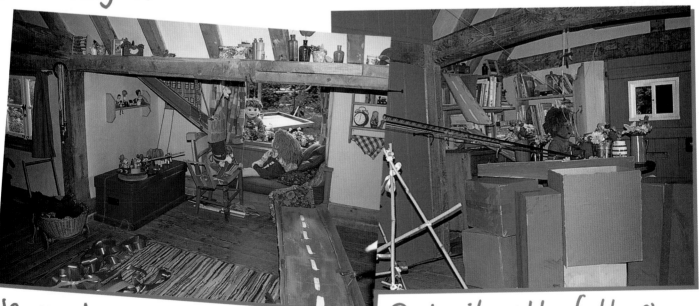

We made a really big machine inside our lovely house.

But it all fell on Tom's head.

29

A Party For Donkey

1. One day Donkey looked a bit fed-up. "Tots!" said Tiny. "What can we do to cheer Donkey up?"

"Let's have a party for Donkey!" said Tom. "We can start by cleaning his shed!"

"Oui," said Tilly.

2. Donkey's shed was very untidy. "Oh la la!" said Tilly. "Poooh!" said Tom.

3. Tiny found the cleaning things in the cupboard under the stairs.

4. The Tots worked hard, they washed and cleaned and cleaned and washed.

5. Tiny made up a cleaning up rhyme:

Donkey we are cheering up,
It's Donkey's party day,
So his shed we're clearing up,
Sweeping up the hay.

6. Just then, Tom noticed something, up on the roof of the shed. Just out o[f] reach, was some untidy straw. "What can we do?" asked Tiny.

7. "J'ai une idée!" said Tilly, and she played a magic tidying tune on her flute.

8. Tom and Tiny sang Tiny's cleaning up rhyme to Tilly's tune.

Donkey we are cheering up,
It's Donkey's party day,
So his shed we're clearing up,
Sweeping up the hay.

9. Furryboo was having a sleep in the straw up on the roof of Donkey's shed. The Tots' special cleaning up song woke Furryboo up.

10. As Furryboo scampered away, all the messy straw floated down on to Tom's head.

11. "Donkey's shed is all clean and lovely," said Tiny, "but now you need to get cleaned up, Tom!"

12. Donkey came to have a look. "Do you like your lovely clean shed?" asked Tiny. "Ee-aw!" said Donkey, and he munched his special cleaning day carrots. "Lovely Donkey!" said Tom.

33

A Rainy Day Party

1. One rainy day, the Tots decided to have a party inside.

2. Tom made some party milkshakes.

3. Tilly decorated the house.

4. Tiny made some party hats.

5. Tom wanted to play some games. Tiny thought it would be fun to play 'Pass The Parcel'.

"But we haven't got any presents," said Tom.

6. "That's all right," said Tiny. "We can use... bananas! When the music stops you have to unwrap the banana!"

7. "Yummy!" said Tom. "I think I like this game!"

Have A Tots Party!

Tiny's stripy jellies

Make one jelly and pour it into several different glasses. Refrigerate until set. Gently pour another flavour on top and refrigerate once again.
Keep going until the glasses are full. You could add fruit into the different layers as well!

"I like the green bit best!"

Tilly's creamy jelly

Melt some jelly in hot water but instead of adding cold water, make your jelly up with milk or evaporated milk and refrigerate until set, as usual. Serve with fresh fruit and whipped cream or plain yogurt.

"Yummy Strawberry!"

Tom's banana milkshakes

Mash a ripe banana in a bowl, using a fork.
Add milk and ice-cream and whisk until smooth.
Ask an adult to pour the milkshake into glasses. It's ready to drink!

For an extra fruity shake, add some melon. Wow!

Tom's wobbly jelly game

When Tilly plays a special wobbly tune on her flute, Tom and Tiny wobble about like jellies. When Tilly stops playing for the count of five, then Tom and Tiny have to stand really still. If one of them wobbles when they should be standing still then the other is the winner. You could play this game with your friends - wobble, wobble, wobble!

"Wobble with Tom!"

Banana ice

Peel a banana and put it in a container without the lid. Ask a grown-up to put it in the freezer for you. After a few hours, your frozen banana is just like ice-cream!

Tilly's hat

1. Cut a strip of card that's long enough to go round your head.

2. Cut strips into the card and roll them over a pencil to make curls.

3. Paste or tape the two ends of the strip together.

4. Decorate your hat with pipe cleaners and buttons. Voilà!

Tom's hat

1. Tom's hat is the same as Tilly's, only cut a zig-zag into the top instead of strips.

Tiny's hat

1. You'll need to cut quite a large semi-circle from paper or card to make a hat like Tiny's.

2. Tape the straight edge together, or ask an adult to staple it for you. This makes your hat into a cone shape.

3. Decorate your hat with ribbons.

Hands off!

Tiny likes to play this game! Put an apple on a paper plate and put it on the floor. Now try and eat the apple without using your hands. See who can eat the most apple.

"It's really difficult!"

Special Secret Hideaway Day

One cloudy day,
Tom was out walking
in the woods. The wind
was sending big,
grey clouds
scurrying across
the sky.

"What a lovely, breezy day
it is today," said Tom, shivering.

Tom sat down on a log for a rest. The birds were singing and a gust of wind rustled through the trees. Just then, Tom noticed something in a pile of leaves by his foot. It was a hedgehog, snuffling its way home.

That gave Tom an idea.

Tilly and Tiny were sharing a book when Tom came into the secret house.

"Tots!" said Tom, unwinding his scarf and unbuttoning his coat, "I've got an idea, I have. But it's going to be a surprise!" Tom ran upstairs.

A little while later, Tom asked the other Tots to "Come and see!"

Tom had made something special out of paper, for the Tots to hide inside.

"This," said Tom, "is my special stay outside day hiding place."

"What's that for, Tom?" asked Tiny.

"It's so we can stay out in the garden and watch all the little animals and things, scurrying about in our lovely garden," said Tom. "Would you like to come inside and have a look?"

"Oui!" said Tilly, and she crawled quickly inside the special hiding place.

"Très bien!" said Tilly.

Then Tiny crawled inside as well.

"Brilliant!" said Tiny. "Clever old Tom."

Even Donkey came to have a look.

Then Tom squeezed himself into the special hiding place.

"Oh dear!" said Tiny as Tom trod on his foot. "Mind my foot!"

"Er, excuse me Tiny, but your elbow is in my face," said Tom.

"Yes, but Tommy Tom, your knee is in my tummy," said Tiny, "Oooff!"

"Oh la la!" said Tilly. "C'est trop petite!"

"Yes, my special hiding place is a bit too small for all three Tots," said Tom.

Just then there was a sudden gust of wind. Whoosh! Tom's special secret hiding place shivered and shook.
"Brrr!" said Tiny.

Woooosh! The wind blew again. Tom's special hiding place shuddered and rattled.
"Brrrrr!" shivered Tom. The Tots held on to one another.

Woooooosh swoosh swoooosh! The wind blew Tom's special stay outside day hiding place right away. Wheeee!
"Oh la la la la la la!" said Tilly.

"It's bigger now!" said Tiny.
"It's a special stay outside day Donkey hiding place," said Tom.
"Ee-aw!" said Donkey.
"Oh dear!" said Tom.

"J'ai une idée!" said Tilly, and she went inside for a minute while Tom and Tiny cleared up.

A little while later, Tiny was watching Tom paint a picture when Tilly called to the other Tots: "Venez voir!"

Tom and Tiny looked at Tilly's special stay outside day blanket hiding place.

"Brilliant!" said Tiny, and he scrambled inside. "Clever old Tilly."

"Lovely," said Tom, as he crawled inside and sat next to Tiny. Then Tilly clambered inside as well. There was plenty of room for all three of the Tots.

Even Donkey came to have a look.

But just then there was a sudden gust of wind. Whoosh! Tilly's special blanket hiding place shivered and shook. But it didn't blow away.

"Oh la la!" said Tilly.

Woooosh! The wind blew again. Tilly's special blanket hiding place shuddered and rattled. But it didn't blow away.

"Oh la la la la!" said Tilly.

Then the wind died down.
    "Phew!" said Tiny.
But then something else happened.

Drip! A raindrop plopped out of the sky. Just one raindrop. Then
one more. Drop! Then another. Drip! And another. Drop!
    "Uh-oh!" said Tom.

Then lots and lots and lots and lots and lots and lots and lots of
raindrops came tumbling out of the sky.
Drip drop! Drip drop! Drip drop! Drip drop! Drip drop!

"Oh non!" said Tilly, as her special blanket stay outside day hiding
place got wetter and wetter.
    "Oh dear, Tots," said Tom, "I think we'd better go inside."

A little while later, Tom and Tilly were
sharing a book when Tiny called: "Come and see!"

"This," said Tiny, "is my special stay inside on a windy, rainy day secret hiding place. Would you like to come inside and have a look?"

"Oui!" said Tilly.

"Yes please, Tiny," said Tom. "What a brilliant idea."

"Oui!" agreed Tilly. "Une idée excellente!"

"Now we can play in our secret den without getting blown away or all soggy, soggy wet!" said Tom.

The Tots liked it so much, they even ate their tea there.

And the rain drip dropped all over the Tots' garden, and the wind blew and blew and blew, rushing around the outside of the Tots' house. Woooooosh swoosh swooooosh! But all three Tots were warm and dry and comfortable in Tiny's special stay inside on a windy, rainy day secret hiding place.

Furryboo came to have a look. He liked it so much, he fell asleep.

Stay Indoors

Have an adventure inside on a rainy day. Make your own secret hideaway.

Put a blanket or a sheet over a table or a couple of chairs. Or you could use a clotheshorse. Take some special things into your tent. Pretend there is a jungle outside, or you're stuck on a snowy mountain. Brrr!

Tilly's Magic Pictures

1. Tom and Tiny
were playing on the swing
when Tilly
called them inside.
"Venez voir!" she said.

2. Inside the house,
Tilly had taped some
sheets of paper on to
the table.
"Regardez!" she said.

3. Tilly rubbed a red
wax crayon over one
of the sheets of paper.
Tom and Tiny
watched closely as
different shapes
began to appear.

4. "Tilly," said Tiny, "is your crayon a special magic crayon?"

"Non," said Tilly. "Voilà!" and she untaped the paper from the table and held it up so Tom and Tiny could see. On the table where the paper had been was a key and a few buttons. And on the paper was an impression of the key and the buttons, made by Tilly's crayon.

5. "Cor!" said Tiny. "That is brilliant!"
"That way of making a picture," explained Tom, "is called rubbing."
"Maintenant, c'est à vous d'essayer," said Tilly.
"Now it's our turn!" said Tiny.

6. Tiny picked up a green crayon and moved round to a fresh piece of paper. "I wonder what will appear in my magic rubbing picture," said Tiny, as he rubbed his crayon over the paper. Gradually, something began to appear. Different kinds of leaves!

47

7. "Brilliant!" said Tiny. "Tilly hid leaves under my paper and now I've made a brilliant leafy magic rubbing picture."

8. Then it was Tom's turn. Tom used a blue crayon. As he rubbed it over the paper, a fork, a spoon, and then some biscuits appeared.

9. "That reminds me," said Tom. "It must be time for tea." "What a brilliant magic rubbing picture surprise," said Tiny, rubbing his tummy and eating a biscuit. "Thank you, Tilly."

l _ _ _ _

l _ _ _ _

C _ _ _ _ _

K _ _ _

b _ _ _ _ _

S _ _ _ _

b _ _ _ _

c _ _ _ _ _

W _ _ _

t _ _ _ _

You can make your own rubbings too.

49

Tom's Special Sky Ship

Tilly and Tiny were sharing a book at the window seat when Tom came inside.

"Come and see!" said Tom, and he led the others into the garden.

Outside the secret house, it was very windy.

"What a lot of windy old wind!" said Tiny, holding his hat on his head to stop it from blowing away.

Tom showed Tilly
and Tiny what he'd been up to all afternoon.
    "I have made a special sky boat!" said Tom,
    "to take all the Tots up into the sky
for a special ride in the clouds!"

Tilly, Tom and Tiny climbed into Tom's sky ship.
    "Here we go, Tots!" said Tom,
and he began to tell a story.

Up, up, up and away
We're flying into the sky
Up, up, up and away
We're flying up ever so high!

The wind's in our sails and it's lifting us up.
Lifting us right off the ground!
Above the cart, the swing
And everything,
The wind is the only sound.

"Wheeee!" said Tiny.
"Wow!" said Tom.
"Oh la la!" said Tilly.
Shshshsh! went the wind.

Up, up, up and away
We're flying into the sky
Up, up, up and away
We're flying up ever so high!

The birds are coming to say "hello"
They've never seen anything like it.
Three Tots floating by,
High up in the sky,
Flying in Tom's special sky ship.

"Wheeee!" said Tiny.
"Wow!" said Tom.
"Oh la la!" said Tilly.
Shshshshshshsh! went the wind.

Up, up, up and away
We're flying into the sky
Up, up, up and away
We're flying up ever so high!

Look down below, our house looks so small.
Tiny says, "It's time to go down!"
With the wind in our hair,
And a second to spare,
We land with a BUMP!
on the ground.

"What a brilliant high up in the sky
pretend flying adventure!" said Tiny,
"Thank you Tom!"
"Oui, merci Tom." said Tilly.

Sky Painting

Back inside the Tots' house Tilly made a special picture of the Tots' sky flying adventure.

1. First of all, Tilly cut some cloud shapes out of paper.

2. Then she put the cloud shapes on piece of white paper. Then she gently covered the whole piece of paper with some blue paint on an old sponge.

3. When Tilly took away the pieces of newspaper, they left white cloud shapes behind.

4. When Tilly's sky painting was dry, she drew all the Tots, and Tom's special sky ship, in crayons on the top.

What would you see if you went up in the sky?

Tilly's Pictures

tom, tiny et moi

Oh la la♪ Banane tom♥

Charmant Donkey

C'est moi Tilly ♪

Shshsh♪ C'est une secret ♡ x

Zippity Zappity Zedd

One day, Tiny decided to be a super hero
- with special magic powers!

Tom was clearing the garden,
He'd been carefully picking up leaves,
He'd swept up some hay in a pile,
Now it was time to give Donkey his tea

When along came Superhero Tiny!
And with a Zippity Zappity Zedd!
Wooooosh!
All the hay that Tom had so carefully swept,
Was scattered all over the shed.

Tilly had lost her favourite teddy,
She couldn't find it anywhere,
She looked in the sink, in the bathroom
And the cupboard under the stairs.

"Oh la la!"

Superhero Tiny came to the rescue!
And with a Zippity Zappity Zedd!
Woooooosh!
Tilly's teddy fell out of a tree,
And landed with a bump on her head!

Tom was hanging out washing,
There was lots and lots and lots,
All those sheets and shirts and trousers,
Some pillow cases, towels and socks.

Superhero Tiny came to help!
And with a Zippity Zappity Zedd!
Wooooosh!
Clean clothes went all over the garden,
"Oh, what a muddle!" Tom said.

All that running around and searching,
Hanging washing out and sweeping up hay,
With all those super superhero adventures
It's been a super exhausting day.

So Tiny's not coming to the rescue!
No Zippity, no zappity, no zedd!
Zzzzzz...
Just the sound of three tired Tots
All sound asleep in their beds!

magine if you had super powers! Where would you
go? What would you do? Would you wear special
clothes?

Draw a picture of what you would look like.

Tots Race Into Space!

The Tots have made space ships and are going to fly to the moon.

To play the Tots' game you need a dice and some counters or buttons. Decide who is going to be Tilly, Tom or Tiny and place the buttons on the starting space. Throw the dice once each, the highest number starts. After that, take turns. The first to reach the Moon wins! Wheeeee, hold on tight!

Stop to look at the house down below. Miss a turn.

"Space bananas!" Stop for a space picnic and miss a turn.

"You big banana!" Tom forgot his crayons. Go back to start.

"Neee-ow!" Tiny's rocket goes super fast! Forward five places.

Tilly plays a magic tune! Sing a song & move forward one place.

Tiny fe say " Dor Say "By and g to s

Tom's special space booster! Roar like a rocket and rush forward two places!

Tilly Start

Tom Start

Tiny Start